W9-BKE-842

# TRISTAN STRONG

## PUNCHES A HOLE IN THE SKY

### THE GRAPHIC NOVEL

ADAPTED BY
**ROBERT VENDITTI**

ILLUSTRATED BY
**OLIVIA STEPHENS**

COLORING BY
**LAURA LANGSTON**

LETTERING BY
**ARIANA MAHER**

BASED ON THE *NEW YORK TIMES* BEST-SELLING NOVEL BY
**KWAME MBALIA**

RICK RIORDAN PRESENTS

DISNEY • HYPERION       LOS ANGELES    NEW YORK

CHAPTER 1

"YOU'LL ONLY BE GONE A MONTH, TRISTAN."

POP

"THE GRIEF COUNSELOR SAID IT WOULD BE GOOD FOR YOU TO GET A CHANGE OF SCENERY."

"YOU HAVEN'T BEEN TO YOUR GRANDPARENTS' FARM IN ALABAMA SINCE YOU WERE LITTLE."

"WHO KNOWS, MAYBE YOU'LL FIND OUT YOU WERE MEANT TO WORK THE LAND."

...EIGHT...

...NINE...

...TEN!

KNOCKOUT!

CAN'T BELIEVE I DROVE ALL THE WAY TO CHICAGO TO SEE A *STRONG* FIGHT SO *SOFT*. THAT'S YOUR *GRANDMOTHER'S* SIDE OF THE FAMILY.

WHEN I WAS YOUR AGE, I'D ALREADY FOUGHT IN TWO *TITLE FIGHTS*. YOUR DAD WAS A *CHAMP*, TOO. WHY, I REMEMBER--

THAT'S ENOUGH, WALTER.

YOU HUNGRY, TRISTAN?

NOT REALLY.

NO, *MA'AM*.

YOU ANSWER *"NO, MA'AM"* TO YOUR GRANDMOTHER, UNDERSTAND?

YEAH.

I MEAN, YES, SIR.

WELL, YOUR MAMA TOLD ME YOU AIN'T BEEN EATING MUCH, AND WE'RE GONNA FIX THAT.

SHE ALSO SAID YOUR COUNSELOR WANTS YOU TO FOCUS ON YOUR WRITING. TO HELP YOU WITH . . . WHAT HAPPENED TO YOUR FRIEND EDDIE.

HMPH. BOY DON'T NEED NO COUNSELOR.

HE NEEDS TO *WORK*. AIN'T NO TIME FOR MOPING WHEN HORSES NEED FEEDING AND FENCES NEED MENDING.

*WALTER!* HE'S HURTING. HE NEEDS--

I KNOW WHAT HE NEEDS!

IS THAT EDDIE'S JOURNAL? THE ONE HE USED TO WRITE IN?

YES, MA'AM. HIS MOM GAVE IT TO ME AT THE FUNERAL. IT HAS ALL HIS *STORIES.* EVEN THE FABLES YOU USED TO TELL US ON YOUR VISITS.

OUR END-OF-YEAR ENGLISH PROJECT WAS SUPPOSED TO BE A COLLECTION OF STORIES FROM OUR CHILDHOOD.

THAT SYMBOL. I HAVEN'T SEEN IT IN A LONG TIME.

YOU KNOW WHAT IT IS?

IT'S THE *SPIDER'S WEB.* AN OLD AFRICAN SYMBOL FOR CREATIVITY AND WISDOM. IT SHOWS HOW TANGLED AND COMPLICATED LIFE CAN BE.

BUT WITH A LITTLE IMAGINATIVE THINKING, WE CAN SOLVE MOST OF OUR PROBLEMS AND THOSE OF OTHERS.

Y'ALL NEED TO STOP FILLING HIS HEAD WITH THAT MESS.

THE BOY NEEDS TO STAY IN THE *REAL WORLD.*

WALTER, DON'T BE SO HARD ON HIM.

BOXING AIN'T GONNA JUST *HAPPEN!* HE GOT TO TRAIN HIS *BODY* AND *MIND!*

FIND IT.

FIND IT!

WE'RE HERE. BEAT SUNDOWN. THAT'S HOW A *STRONG* DOES IT.

WHAT'S IN THOSE TREES OVER THERE? IT LOOKS LIKE SOMETHING'S SHINING.

A *BOTTLE TREE*. SLAVES CARRIED THE PRACTICE OVER WITH THEM FROM AFRICA AS A WAY TO CAPTURE AND DISPOSE OF ANY *HAINTS* WANDERING AROUND.

HAINTS?

*EVIL SPIRITS.*

I DON'T WANT YOU MESSING AROUND OVER THERE. THEM OLD TREES AREN'T FOR PLAYING ON.

IT WAS A LONG DRIVE. I'LL FIX YOU SOME DINNER, SWEETIE.

CLOAKS OFF, EVERYONE. WE NEED *SPEED*, NOT STEALTH.

WHO--?

HOW--?

*BRER FOX* IS THE NAME.

HOLD UP. *BRER FOX?* FROM THE *STORY* MY NANA USED TO TELL ME AND MY FRIEND EDDIE?

THERE WAS A FOX AND A BEAR TRYING TO EAT A RABBIT, BUT THE RABBIT WAS TOO *SMART* AND ALWAYS GOT AWAY.

TOO SMART. ǝCHFFǝ THAT'LL BE THE DAY.

YOU'RE IN *ALKE*, TRISTAN. THIS WORLD IS THE DREAM TO YOUR WORLD'S REALITY. THE TALES AND FABLES YOU THINK ARE MADE UP?

THEY *EXIST* HERE. AND THAT HOLE IN THE SKY IS CAUSING CREATURES FAR WORSE THAN BONE SHIPS TO GO INTO A FRENZY.

SO THAT'S *ENOUGH* QUESTIONS.

RIGHT NOW? BE READY TO RUN.

BY THE WAY, YOUR POCKET IS GLOWING.

FETTERLINGS!

THANKS FOR THE *BOOK*, BOY.

OH, YOU'RE AWAKE!

GOOD! THEY WERE GETTING WORRIED.

I'M *CHESTNUTT*. I'M SUPPOSED TO COME FETCH YOU. THEY HAVE TO DECIDE WHO'S GOING TO GO.

NO, WAIT, FIRST THEY HAVE TO SEE IF WE'RE GOING TO GO, AND THEN, IF YES, *WHO'S* GOING TO GO.

I HOPE IT'S ME.

*COME ON!* WE HAVE TO HURRY!

WHAT *IS* THIS PLACE?

YOU'RE IN *THE THICKET.*

IS IT SOME SORT OF HIDEOUT?

YUP, YUP! ONCE THE *IRON MONSTERS* STARTED TERRORIZING US, JOHN HENRY CONVINCED BRER RABBIT TO USE THE THICKET AS A *REFUGE.* BUT IF SOMEONE IS TOO SICK OR TOO LITTLE TO GET HERE, WE HAVE TO GO FIND THEM.

THAT'S HOW I GOT HERE. *BRER FOX* RESCUED ME WHEN I WAS A BABY. A COUPLE OF THOSE MONSTERS ATTACKED MY FAMILY'S BURROW. I WAS THE ONLY ONE LEFT.

IT'S NOT YOUR FAULT, YOU KNOW, WHAT HAPPENED TO BRER FOX.

IF I'D BEEN *QUICKER* OR *STRONGER,* I MIGHT'VE BEEN ABLE TO SAVE HIM. ALL I DO IS LOSE.

I...I'M SORRY.

BRER FOX TOLD ME WE CAN'T HARP ON PAST MISTAKES. HE WAS ALWAYS TELLING ME STUFF LIKE THAT.

I KNOW YOU TRIED, AND I KNOW WHAT BRER FOX DID, AND I KNOW HE'S GONE.

BUT AS LONG AS I HAVE HIS WORDS, I'LL HAVE HIM.

SO IT'S OKAY.

THANKS FOR THE *BOOK,* BOY.

*TRISTAN! HURRY!*

JOHN HENRY!

YOU'RE MY *FAVORITE* FOLKTALE!

HOW YOU *HAMMERED SPIKES* FOR THE RAILROAD FROM MORNING TO NIGHT!

YOU EVEN RACED A *STEAM DRILL* AND *WON!*

MY GRANDMOTHER SAYS THERE WAS *MORE* TO THE STORY. STUFF LEFT OUT OF THE HISTORY BOOKS. LIKE WHEN *SLAVERY* WAS BANNED, THE PLANTATION OWNERS DIDN'T WANT TO HAVE TO PAY THE SLAVES.

SO THEY MADE *LAWS,* AND WHEN THE SLAVES BROKE THEM, THEY MADE THEM DO THE SAME WORK THEY ALWAYS DID. FOR FREE.

THAT'S RIGHT, TRISTAN. I *AM* JOHN HENRY.

THIS IS MISS SARAH AND MISS ROSE. AND *BRER RABBIT,* OF COURSE.

SO *THIS* IS THE BOY RESPONSIBLE FOR THE END OF THE WORLD.

WHAT BRER MEANS TO SAY--

--IS THAT YOU HAVE SOME *EXPLAINING* TO DO, AND QUICKLY.

YOU HAVE. . . WINGS.

"THEY SAY THE PEOPLE COULD FLY."

YOUR GRANDMOTHER TOLD YOU THAT, TOO, DID SHE? HOW IN AFRICA, OUR PEOPLE FLEW ALL THE TIME?

THAT WAS BEFORE SLAVERY.

THEN CAME THE *CHAINS* AND *SHIPS,* THE *PAIN* AND *WHIPS,* AND THE PEOPLE'S WINGS FELL OR WERE TORN OFF.

IT SEEMS WE HAVE A *STORYTELLER* HERE, ROSE.

ENOUGH *NICETIES.* I'D LIKE TO KNOW JUST *WHAT* THE TWO OF YOU WERE THINKING.

WHO TWO?

HEY, BUMBLE-TONGUE.

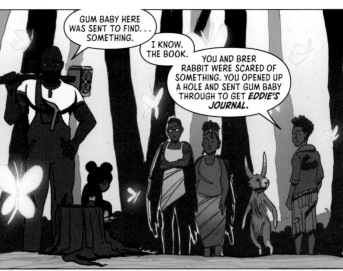

GUM BABY HERE WAS SENT TO FIND... SOMETHING.

I KNOW. THE BOOK. YOU AND BRER RABBIT WERE SCARED OF SOMETHING. YOU OPENED UP A HOLE AND SENT GUM BABY THROUGH TO GET *EDDIE'S JOURNAL.*

*SPY!* HOW DO *YOU* KNOW ABOUT OUR *PLAN?*

I DIDN'T SPY ON ANYONE. I SAW IT WHEN I OPENED THE JOURNAL.

THIS JOURNAL... DID IT HAVE A SYMBOL ON IT?

MY GRANDMOTHER SAID IT WAS AN OLD AFRICAN SYMBOL FOR A SPIDERWEB. SOMETHING ABOUT BEING CREATIVE.

AND LATELY, SINCE MY FRIEND DIED, IT'S BEEN *GLOWING* SOMETIMES.

*I KNEW IT! I KNEW IT!* DIDN'T I *TELL* YOU, JOHNNY MY BOY? I SAID WE'D FIND IT, AND WE *DID!* TOOK A BIT *LONGER* THAN EXPECTED, BUT WE *FOUND* IT!

WHY *DID* IT TAKE SO LONG?

GUM BABY SAID IN HER REPORT THAT SHE THOUGHT SHE WAS ONLY GONE FOR AN HOUR OR TWO, BUT IT WAS A *YEAR*.

AND THE *FLAMING TEAR* IN THE SKY--DOES THAT HAVE ANYTHING TO DO WITH WHAT'S BEEN HAPPENING?

IT'S SIMPLE *TIME DISTORTION*, JOHN. VARIOUS REALMS EXPERIENCE TIME DIFFERENTLY. WITHOUT PROPER PRECAUTIONS, SOMEONE COULD LIVE A *LIFETIME* IN ONE WORLD AND ONLY A *MOMENT* IN THE OTHER.

BUT YOU'RE MISSING THE *BIGGER* PICTURE. WE CAN *FIX* THE TEAR AND EVERYTHING ELSE ONCE WE HAVE THE *BOOK*.

THAT'S IT THEN. *HAND OVER* THE BOOK.

GIVE US ANANSI'S STORIES.

*ANANSI?* NO, IT WAS EDDIE'S JOURNAL.

*NO,* IT CONTAINS THE *SPIDER GOD'S* STORIES. ANANSI, WHO TRICKED THE SKY GOD NYAME INTO GIVING HIM THE *FIRST* STORIES.

ANANSI, THE *GREATEST STORYTELLER* TO EVER ENTERTAIN.

THE BOOK IS MORE THAN YOU THINK, TRISTAN. IT'S THE *KEY* TO EVERYTHING.

NOW HAND IT OVER.

I SORT OF... LOST IT.

FIGHTING WITH GUM BABY, DAMAGING A BOTTLE TREE, RIPPING THE FABRIC BETWEEN WORLDS, AND NOW *THIS*?

IT'S *BAD ENOUGH* THE OTHER ALKEANS WON'T TALK TO US.

NO, NO, NO! WE'RE DOOMED! *DOOMED!*

TO THINK WE GAVE YOU ANOTHER CHANCE. AND *THIS* IS HOW YOU COMPLETE YOUR MISSION?

*SHAMEFUL!* MAYBE SHE'LL NEVER BE READY.

WILL YOU ALL JUST TELL ME HOW TO GET BACK *HOME?*

YOU THINK YOU CAN JUST *DISAPPEAR* AFTER ALL THE TROUBLE YOU'VE CAUSED? UPSETTING THE BALANCE BETWEEN WORLDS LIKE A *LITTLE PUNK?*

I'VE *SEEN* YOUR TYPE BEFORE. NO RESPECT. WILD AND UNCARING. AND--WORST OF ALL--YOU *CONSISTENTLY* LET OTHERS DOWN.

YOU DON'T KNOW *ANYTHING.* YOU SENT SOMEBODY TO STEAL FROM ME BECAUSE YOU WANTED SOMETHING. BUT DID YOU SEE THAT I HAD LOST MY *BEST FRIEND?*

THAT ALL I HAD LEFT OF HIM WAS THE *JOURNAL* WE WORKED ON TOGETHER, COLLECTING STORIES?

CAN YOU *PICTURE* A BOY IN A *STRANGE PLACE,* AND THAT JOURNAL IS THE *ONLY THING* REMINDING HIM OF *HOME* AND *GOOD TIMES?*

AND SOMEONE TRIES TO *STEAL* THE *ONLY* GOOD THING THAT BOY HAS LEFT?

CAN YOU PICTURE IT?

"ANANSESEM"? WHAT'S THAT?

IT MEANS YOU'RE A *STORYTELLER.* BUT MORE THAN JUST WORDS. MORE THAN JUST "ONCE UPON A TIME" AND "THE END."

IT'S ABOUT THE ENTIRE *EXPERIENCE,* FROM THE AUDIENCE TO THE STAGE TO THE SPECTACLE.

ENOUGH!

OF ALL THE *BRAINLESS, SELFISH*--

BRER!

THAT'S *ENOUGH* OUT OF *YOU!*

IS IT NOW?

THEN YOU KNOW WHERE TO FIND ME.

BRER WILL BE FINE. WHAT'S IMPORTANT IS WHAT HAPPENS *NEXT.* THE IRON MONSTERS ARE *HUNTING* US FOR SOME REASON. PICKING US OFF ONE BY ONE.

EVERYONE WHO'S CAUGHT GETS DRAGGED TO. . .

. . .WELL, TO A *BAD* PLACE, NEVER TO BE SEEN AGAIN.

YOU MEAN THE *MAAFA*--

ZIP IT, BUMBLE-TONGUE!

WE TRY NOT TO CALL ATTENTION TO THAT *THING.*

AND YOU IN PARTICULAR NEED TO BE CAREFUL. YOU HAVE *ANANSI'S GIFT.* WHEN YOU TELL STORIES, SOMETHING SPECIAL HAPPENS.

THE WORLD LISTENS TO YOU. AND YOU LISTEN TO IT.

IT'S A LOT TO TAKE IN, TRISTAN. THAT'S ENOUGH FOR NOW. WE NEED TO DO SOME FIGURING ABOUT THIS.

GUM BABY, TAKE TRISTAN TO GET SOME FOOD.

WHAM

HEY, NIMROD. YOU'RE TALKING TO THE WRONG ONE.

EDDIE? IS THAT YOU?

YOU'RE TALKING TO THE **WRONG** ONE.

**EDDIE!**

WHERE ARE YOU?!

EDDIE!

"JOHN IS WAITING FOR YOU."

THESE IRON MONSTERS ARE KILLING US SLOWLY, TRISTAN.

BUT YOU'RE *JOHN HENRY.* YOU'RE ALL *GODS.*

THEY'RE SMARTER THAN THEY USED TO BE. THEIR LEADER IS *DEVIOUS* IN WAYS WE NEVER COULD'VE IMAGINED.

WHO *IS* THE MAA--

I MEAN, THEIR LEADER.

IT AIN'T REALLY A *WHO.* IT'S MORE A *FEELING.* OF DEVASTATION AND DESTRUCTION. HUNGER AND GREED.

IT'S *PAIN* AND WHAT IT SURVIVES ON.

"IT CAME HERE WITH THE FIRST OF US, WITH ME AND BRER RABBIT AND BRER FOX AND THE FLYING LADIES.

"IT'S THE *SADNESS* TO OUR JOY."

WE MANAGED TO DEFEAT IT ONCE. SENT IT TO THE BOTTOM OF THE BURNING SEA. BUT SOMETHING'S BROUGHT IT TO THE SURFACE AGAIN, AND IT'S SENDING *EVERY MONSTER* IT HAS AT US.

BRER SAYS HE HAS A PLAN. AND YOU'RE PART OF IT.

ME? BUT...

I WISH WE COULD KEEP YOU OUT OF IT, BUT I DON'T SEE HOW WE HAVE A CHOICE. WE NEED YOUR HELP.

AN ANANSESEM IS SPECIAL. THE LEGENDS, THE FABLES, ALL THE TALES YOU HEARD GROWING UP-- THEY'RE LIKE *FUEL* FOR US FOLK HEROES.

AND WHEN AN ANANSESEM TELLS THEM, THEY'RE EVEN MORE POWERFUL. YOU CARRY THE STORIES THAT BROUGHT US HERE. STORIES FROM YOUR WORLD AND MINE.

WHAT'S THE PLAN?

IN HERE.

MM-HMM.

GOT IT.

PASS IT ALONG.

THIS IS THE **WARREN.** THEM LITTLE HOLES ARE TUNNELS THAT LEAD ALL OVER MIDPASS. A FEW OF 'EM GO CLEAR OVER TO THE MAINLAND.

THE WARREN SOCIETY GATHERS **INFORMATION** AND BRINGS IT BACK TO BRER, WHERE HE ORGANIZES IT AND FILES IT AWAY FOR FUTURE REFERENCE.

SO THEN, WHAT'S THE PLAN, BRER?

FROM WHAT I'VE BEEN ABLE TO GATHER, THERE'S SOME CONNECTION BETWEEN THE **BURNING TEAR** IN THE SKY AND THE **IRON MONSTERS.** I DON'T KNOW WHAT.

WHAT I DO KNOW IS THAT WHEN YOUNG **FISTICUFFS** HERE BATTERED THE POOR BOTTLE TREE, THAT **UPSET** SOMETHING.

SO, IF WE CAN PUSH THE BOY BACK THROUGH AND CLOSE THE HOLE BEHIND HIM, IT STANDS TO REASON WHATEVER IS **AGGRAVATING** THINGS WILL BE CUT OFF.

THAT'S ALL WELL AND GOOD, BUT SOMEONE NEEDS TO GET UP THERE.

AND WE AREN'T TRYING AGAIN. MY WINGS STILL TWINGE FROM THE **HEAT.**

ONLY **ONE** PERSON CAN FIX THE RIP IN THE SKY AND PERHAPS GET RID OF OUR UNWELCOME GUESTS.

**ANANSI.**

KWAKU ANANSI HASN'T BEEN SEEN IN MONTHS.

IF WE COULD *FIND* HIM, THOUGH. . .

IT AIN'T HAPPENIN'. IT JUST *AIN'T*.

EVEN IF HE WASN'T *LONG GONE*, HIDING SOMEWHERE, WHAT MAKES YOU THINK AN ALKEAN GOD IS GONNA HELP US MIDPASS GODS?

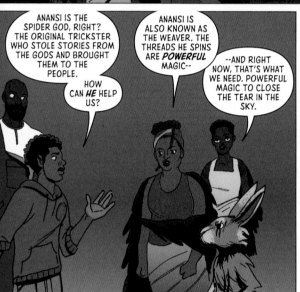

ANANSI IS THE SPIDER GOD, RIGHT? THE ORIGINAL TRICKSTER WHO STOLE STORIES FROM THE GODS AND BROUGHT THEM TO THE PEOPLE.

HOW CAN *HE* HELP US?

ANANSI IS ALSO KNOWN AS THE WEAVER. THE THREADS HE SPINS ARE *POWERFUL* MAGIC--

--AND RIGHT NOW, THAT'S WHAT WE NEED. POWERFUL MAGIC TO CLOSE THE TEAR IN THE SKY.

EVEN IF WE FIND HIM, HIS HELP COMES AT A *STEEP* PRICE.

WE'LL HAVE TO OFFER SOMETHING MIGHTY VALUABLE TO LURE HIM OUT AND OVER TO OUR SIDE. PERHAPS THE *MOST VALUABLE* THING OF ALL.

THE *STORY BOX*.

NO. IT'S *TOO DANGEROUS*.

A STORY WHAT?

THE *STORY BOX*. A TREASURE VAULT FOR TALES AND BALLADS. SOME OLDER THAN THE SUN, OTHERS NO ONE HAS HEARD BEFORE.

THERE ARE MANY, BUT THE ORIGINAL-- THE *TRUE* STORY BOX--THE ONE ANANSI OUTSMARTED NYAME TO GET. . . IS UNIQUE.

BUT IF HE ALREADY HAS IT...

HE DOESN'T. ANANSI AND I WERE WORKING TOGETHER ON A WAY TO STOP THE IRON MONSTERS. STUDYING THE STORY BOX'S MAGIC TO SEE IF IT COULD HELP.

BUT WE WERE ATTACKED, AND WE HAD TO *ABANDON* THE BOX. ANANSI DISAPPEARED, BUT THE BOX IS WAITING RIGHT WHERE WE LEFT IT.

IN THE *GOLDEN CRESCENT.*

THE POWER IN THAT STORY BOX... IT'S THE ONE THING THAT COULD GIVE US A FIGHTING CHANCE.

IF WE DO THIS... HOW?

WE USE THE *BUTTERFLY WHISPERER.* A STORY BOX IS A VESSEL FOR MAGIC STORIES, RIGHT? IT HOLDS THEM, READY TO BRING THEM TO LIFE. LIKE AN ANANSESEM WOULD.

IF HE SPINS ONE OF HIS TALES IN THE BOX'S VICINITY, IT'LL LEAD US STRAIGHT TO IT. WE TAKE IT, AND ANANSI WILL COME TO US TO GET IT BACK.

I HATE TO SAY IT...

...BUT IT MIGHT BE OUR ONLY OPTION.

SO, TRISTAN, YOU READY TO BE A HERO?

NO.

ONE OF SIS CROW'S BROOD SPOTTED THIS. THEY ALWAYS HAVE AN EYE FOR SOMETHING SHINY.

I THOUGHT YOU MIGHT WANT IT.

MAYBE IT HELPS A LITTLE. THAT SYMBOL IS AN *ADINKRA.* SYMBOLS LIKE THAT HELD GREAT MEANING FOR THE PEOPLE WHO WORE THEM.

IF IT CAME OFF YOUR FRIEND'S BOOK-- THE ONE ALL THIS *HOOPLA* IS ABOUT--I EXPECT YOU MIGHT WANT TO HOLD ON TO IT.

THANK YOU, JOHN.

REALLY. THANK YOU.

OUCH! IT *BURNS!* WHY--?

THEM *IRON MONSTERS* ARE COMING.

SKREEEEE!

PUT THESE ON.

YOU CAN GO BACK IF YOU WANT. INTO THE TUNNELS, WHERE IT'S SAFE.

WE SHOULD BACK UP TO THE ENTRANCE. IN CASE ONE GETS PAST US.

*NOTHING'S* GETTING PAST US.

CHAPTER 3

CHESTNUTT, KEEP AN EYE OUT FOR **BRAND FLIES.**

AYE-AYE.

BRAND FLIES? I DON'T LIKE THE SOUND OF THAT.

YOU'RE AFRAID OF **BUGS,** TOO?

NO. MAYBE.

I DON'T LIKE **HEIGHTS.**

SORRY. I NEED TO STAY AT HIGH ALTITUDE TO USE THE CLOUD COVER.

S'OKAY.

WHAT ARE **YOU** AFRAID OF, AYANNA?

SURPRISES.

RUSTLE

RUSTLE

AAAA! FETTERLING!

FETTERLING?

WHERE?!

GUM BABY! **WHAT** ARE YOU **DOING** HERE?

WHAT'S GUM BABY DOING HERE?

HOW **DARE** YOU LEAVE ON A MISSION **WITHOUT** GUM BABY! THAT'S LIKE LEAVING **SAND** OUT OF A **SANDWICH!**

YOU'RE **SUPPOSED** TO BE ON KITCHEN DUTY.

GUM BABY THOUGHT IF SHE GOT ANOTHER CHANCE, SHE COULD PROVE SHE CAN BE PART OF THE TEAM.

THEN GUM BABY COULD LIVE HER DREAM.

GUM BABY WANTS TO BE A **PILOT** LIKE AYANNA.

DON'T BE **WHISPERING** ABOUT GUM BABY!

GUM BABY **FINALLY** GOT A MISSION, AND IF SHE DID IT RIGHT, GUM BABY WOULD'VE BEEN A PILOT.

BUMBLE-TONGUE RUINED **EVERYTHING!**

HOW **DID** YOU AND GUM BABY END UP DESTROYING THE LIVES OF **EVERYONE** IN MIDPASS AND POSSIBLY ALKE AS WELL?

YOU TELL IT, BUMBLETONGUE. IT'S HURTS GUM BABY TOO MUCH.

A STORY! A STORY!

"THE *GOLDEN CRESCENT.*"

IT'S. . .

*BEAUTIFUL.*

THESE STATUES LOOK SO *REAL.* THEY GIVE GUM BABY THE HEEBIE-JEEBIES.

QUIT PLAYING AROUND, GUM BABY, AND GET OVER HERE. I THINK WE FOUND SOMETHING.

YUP, YUP! IT MIGHT BE A DOOR.

YOU THINK THE STORY BOX IS IN THERE? COULD IT REALLY BE THAT EASY?

THERE'S NO HANDLE. I DON'T SEE A WAY TO OPEN IT.

REMEMBER WHAT BRER RABBIT SAID? WHEN THE ANANSESEM TELLS A STORY--

--IT'LL BE *DRAWN* TO THE STORY BOX.

I GUESS I'LL GIVE IT A SHOT.

WHAT IF I TOLD YOU STORIES DIDN'T ALWAYS *EXIST.*

LEAVE!

HNAGH!

TRISTAN? WHAT'S WRONG?

MY HEAD. YOU DON'T FEEL IT? I--

THEY CANNOT HEAR ME. BUT *YOU* CAN. WHY?

WHY ARE YOU *HERE?*

HAVE YOU COME TO *TORMENT* ME FURTHER? DOES YOUR MASTER NEED MORE OF MY *PAIN?*

WERE MY *PEOPLE,* MY *HEART,* MY *HOME* NOT ENOUGH?

MY LORD, WE'RE NOT HERE TO HURT YOU.

*WHO* ARE YOU TALKING TO?

THE STATUE. IT *ISN'T* A STATUE.

OH NO. THE CHAINS. THEY'RE *FETTERLINGS.*

AND AROUND HIS HEAD. . .

. . .THOSE ARE *BRAND FLIES.*

NYAME IS TOO POWERFUL TO BE KILLED BY THEIR STINGS, BUT THEIR POISON IS KEEPING HIM *PARALYZED.*

ALL THE ALKEAN PEOPLE. . . THEY WERE TAKEN. NYAME COULDN'T DO ANYTHING BUT WATCH.

*I* CAN DO SOMETHING.

ANANSI TRICKED *PYTHON* NEXT. HE DARED HIM TO MEASURE HIMSELF AGAINST A POLE...

...THEN TIED PYTHON TO IT AND CARRIED HIM AWAY. BUT ANANSI STILL WASN'T DONE.

TRISTAN, WHAT ARE YOU DOING?

NANA LOVED TELLING THIS STORY. IT WAS THE FIRST ONE EDDIE WROTE IN HIS JOURNAL.

THE IRON MONSTERS ARE *ATTRACTED* TO STORIES, RIGHT? *SO* I'M DRAWING THEM AWAY FROM NYAME.

GOOD JOB. WHAT DO WE DO NOW?

RUN, I GUESS?

YOU *GUESS?*

RUN!

I KNOW WHY YOU ARE HERE, ANANSESEM. YOU COME FOR THE STORY BOX, WITH THE HOPE *ANANSI* WILL AID YOU.

AND YOU THINK I SHOULD HELP YOU IN EXCHANGE FOR YOUR EFFORTS JUST NOW? YOU HAVE MY THANKS. BUT MY *SUPPORT* IS ANOTHER MATTER.

MIDPASS IS *DYING,* LORD NYAME--

*EVERYONE* IS DYING! THE MONSTERS TOOK *ALL* MY PEOPLE TO *DIE!*

THEY'RE NOT DEAD. I SAW THEM IN A DREAM. OR MAYBE A VISION. I DIDN'T UNDERSTAND IT AT FIRST, BUT I DO NOW. THEY'RE BEING *HELD* SOMEWHERE.

HOW *LONG* HAVE YOU KNOWN THIS?!

I'M SORRY. I SHOULD'VE SAID SOMETHING.

IT MATTERS NOT.

YOU ARE NOT THE FIRST USURPER TO COME HERE, NOR THE SECOND. IT IS I WHO AM SORRY--

--BUT YOU WILL NEED A NEW PLAN.

THE STORY BOX IS . . . *GONE?*

YOU KNOW ABOUT US ALREADY. OUR PLANS TO BARTER WITH ANANSI TO CLOSE THE TEAR IN THE SKY.

I DO.

I'M A *GOD.*

I'D FIX THE TEAR MYSELF, BUT MUCH OF MY POWER HAS BEEN SAPPED.

IT WILL BE SOME TIME BEFORE I AM MYSELF. I MAY NOT BE ABLE TO GIVE YOU THE HELP YOU SEEK.

BUT I CAN GIVE YOU SOMETHING ELSE.

*GYE NYAME.*

SO YOU KNOW MY *ADINKRA*? GOOD. YOUR *BRACELET*, PLEASE.

YOU ALREADY HAVE ANANSI'S ADINKRA, WHICH BRINGS POWER TO YOUR STORIES. THAT IS IMPORTANT, BECAUSE ALKE IS *WOVEN* WITH STORIES, AND THE THREADS EXIST ALL AROUND US.

THIS CHARM WILL BRING FOCUS TO YOUR SURROUNDINGS AND HELP YOU GAIN *CLARITY*.

YOU'LL FIND THE *ILLUSIONS* OF ALKE A BIT. . .EASIER TO SEE THROUGH.

WHAT I TELL YOU NOW IS ALSO IMPORTANT. ALKE IS A LAND *DIVIDED*. THE GREAT CITIES DO NOT SHARE AS THEY ONCE DID.

THE IRON MONSTERS ONLY PUSHED A WEDGE INTO A *FRACTURED* LANDSCAPE THAT ALREADY EXISTED.

I AGREE WITH YOUR GOAL, IF NOT YOUR PLAN. ANANSI, IF HE CAN BE FOUND AND BRIBED, COULD WEAVE THE TEAR SHUT AND GREATLY DIMINISH THE POWER OF THE IRON MONSTERS.

BUT THEY WILL STILL NEED TO BE *DEFEATED* ONCE AND FOR ALL.

PILOT, DO YOU KNOW THE RIDGEFOLK OF *ISIHLANGU?*

YES, BUT IT'S A *FORTRESS*. THEY *REALLY* DON'T LIKE VISITORS. WE CAN'T--

IF YOU SEEK A *CLUE* ABOUT MY STORY BOX, I WOULD START THERE.

REMEMBER THIS: THOSE WHO HELP YOU MAY NOT BE ON YOUR SIDE, AND THOSE WHO OPPOSE YOU CAN BE YOUR GREATEST ALLIES.

LIKE. . .CAN YOU ELABORATE?

CAN'T WE GET A CLEAR INSTRUCTION OR SOMETHING? A MANUAL? A STEP-BY-STEP GUIDE TO BEING A HERO?

THAT IS NOT HOW THIS WORKS. HEROES DON'T--

WE'RE NOT HEROES. WE'RE A CREW STRAIGHT OUT OF A DUSTY FAIRY-TALE BOOK.

EVERYONE EXPECTS ME TO CONFRONT *BEASTS* AND *MONSTERS* AND FLY AROUND ON A RAFT. I DON'T EVEN LIKE FLYING. I'M *SCARED* OF HEIGHTS. THERE, I SAID IT--

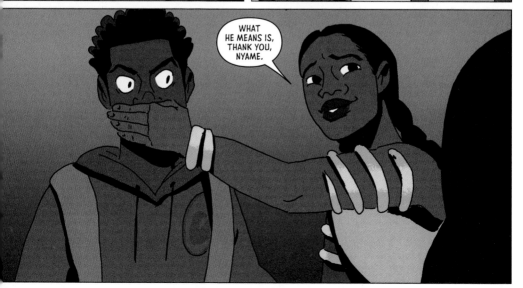

WHAT HE MEANS IS, THANK YOU, NYAME.

"WE'LL GO TO ISIHLANGU."

YOU STILL THINK HIDING IN THE *TRASH CAR* WAS A GOOD IDEA?

WE MADE IT *INSIDE*, DIDN'T WE?

THIS IS *INCREDIBLE*. NO RABBIT HAS EVER MADE IT THIS FAR. IF I CAN BRING NEW INFORMATION ABOUT THE RIDGE BACK TO THE WARREN SOCIETY...

...THEY'LL *HAVE* TO MAKE ME A MEMBER.

WHILE Y'ALL WERE *JAWING*, GUM BABY FOUND A BACK DOOR.

MOVE!

THERE'S A WHOLE *CITY* INSIDE THIS MOUNTAIN.

THERE ARE RUMORS IN THE WARREN SOCIETY ENCYCLOPEDIAS. THEY SAY THE RIDGEFOLK HAVE A *VAULT* WHERE THEY KEEP THEIR MOST VALUABLE ITEMS.

IF THE STORY BOX IS ANYWHERE AROUND HERE, IT'S THERE. YUP, YUP.

*THERE.* THE ROOM ALL THE WAY AT THE TOP.

THAT HAS TO BE IT.

HARDEST PLACE TO REACH, RIGHT?

ALL RIGHT, *SNATCH-AND-GRAB* TIME.

WE FIND THE STORY BOX, AND WE'RE OUT. THEY'LL NEVER KNOW WE WERE--

*THIEVES.* YOU BRING THE *WRATH* OF ISIHLANGU ON YOURSELVES.

THEY'VE HAD LOVED ONES STOLEN, TOO. JUST LIKE *MIDPASS* AND THE *GOLDEN CRESCENT*.

IF THE IRON MONSTERS CAN REACH EVEN HERE, *NO PLACE* IS SAFE.

I'LL HANDLE THIS.

MAKE YOUR NEXT MOVE VERY *SLOWLY*, THIEF.

GREAT ELDER GHOST GUY? WHAT IF I TOLD YOU *ALL* THE LANDS OF ALKE ARE UNDER THE SAME THREAT?

THAT BECAUSE NO ONE TALKED WITH EACH OTHER, AND YOU ALL CLOSED YOUR BORDERS, YOU *FAILED* TO PROTECT EVERYTHING YOU LOVE.

LET ME TELL YOU A *STORY*.

THIS ONE HAS THE BLESSING OF THE *GODS*, ELDER FEZILE.

IF HE SPEAKS, ISIHLANGU SHOULD LISTEN.

VERY WELL.

DON'T DO TOO MUCH.

NAW, BUMBLETONGUE. YOU GO AHEAD AND DO THE *MOST*.

ANANSI WALTZED IN HERE, WITH HIS *CHARM* AND HIS *COMPLIMENTS* AND PRESENTED THE STORY BOX TO US. HE SAID IT WAS A *GIFT* FOR BETTER RELATIONS.

BUT IT WAS A *TRICK.* HE WANTED TO HIDE IT HERE, SO HE COULD RUN AWAY.

HONORED ANCESTORS, WE HAVE ALL WITNESSED THAT THIS BOY HAS THE *STORYTELLER'S GIFT.*

IT'S "TRISTAN."

LET THE WARRIORS OF MIDPASS TAKE BACK THE STORY BOX, FIND ANANSI, AND MAKE OUR HOMES *SAFE* AGAIN.

WHAT ARE THEY WHISPERING ABOUT?

PROBABLY DECIDING WHETHER THEY WANT TO LISTEN TO A BUNCH OF KIDS.

*GROWN-UPS,* AM I RIGHT?

TRISTAN.

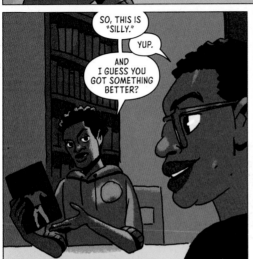

SO, THIS IS "SILLY."

YUP.

AND I GUESS YOU GOT SOMETHING BETTER?

ONLY THE STRONGEST, SMOOTHEST, *WILDEST* HERO EVER. RIDES A CROW THE SIZE OF A CADILLAC TRUCK--NO, A *STRETCH LIMO!*

HE EVEN HAS HIS OWN WALK-UP MUSIC--THEY SAY DRUMS PLAY WHEN HE WALKS. HIS WALK IS *RHYTHM* AND HIS WORDS ARE *PRIDE!*

HE USED TO BE A PRINCE. IN AFRICA. BUT HE GOT CAPTURED AND WAS FORCED INTO SLAVERY. HIS NAME--

--IS *HIGH JOHN.*

MY GRANDMOTHER TELLS ME ALL THOSE STORIES.

YO, THAT'S *SO COOL!* YOU KNOW THOSE AREN'T WRITTEN DOWN ANYWHERE? THEY WERE PASSED ALONG BY WORD OF MOUTH.

I'VE BEEN TRYING TO COLLECT OLD FOLKTALES AND STUFF. I WRITE THEM DOWN IN MY *JOURNAL.*

DO YOU THINK YOUR GRANDMOTHER WOULD TELL ME SOME STORIES?

GIRL, PLEASE. GUM BABY MEANS WE'RE GLAD TO HAVE YOU. WE NEED ALL THE HELP WE CAN GET.

I SHALL BE COMING WITH YOU. ANANSI OWES ALL OF ISIHLANGU AN *EXPLANATION.*

AND I WILL SHOW YOU MIDFOLK HOW TO FIGHT, OF COURSE.

NOW TAKE THE STORY BOX. I HOPE YOUR PLAN SUCCEEDS.

FOR *ALL* OUR SAKES.

WHAT SORT OF SOGGY GARBAGE IS THIS MESS?

YEAH, Y'ALL CAN KEEP THAT. I'M OFF ON OLD FAMILIAR.

YOU DIDN'T KNOW?

THIS IS HOW ANANSI BROUGHT IT TO US. IT'S *EMPTY.*

I NEED A MOMENT HERE.

HOW DID YOU NOT KNOW NYAME'S STORY BOX WAS EMPTY?

WE NEVER THOUGHT TO ASK.

IT'S NOT LIKE WE *COULD* ASK.

THE QUESTION IS, WHAT DO WE DO *NOW?*

I THINK WE TAKE IT TO BRER RABBIT ANYWAY, LIKE WE'RE SUPPOSED TO. MAYBE IT WILL STILL BRING ANANSI...

YOU THINK ANANSI WILL BARTER FOR A BROKEN, DUSTY OLD CRATE?

WHAT IF YOU HAD IT *REPAIRED?*

IT WAS NYAME'S CREATION IN THE FIRST PLACE. SURELY HE COULD RESTORE IT. MAYBE EVEN REFILL IT WITH STORIES.

THEN YOU TAKE IT ON TO MIDPASS AND SUMMON ANANSI.

LIKE YOU SAID, THERE'S NO POINT IN BRINGING AN EMPTY, BROKEN STORY BOX.

OKAY, YES, LET'S GET IT FIXED. NYAME OWES US ONE ANYWAY FOR FREEING HIM FROM *IRON-MONSTER* CONTROL.

BEFORE YOU EMBARK, TRISTAN, WALK WITH ME.

CHAPTER 5

CHESTNUTT WAS STUNG, TOO. POOR THING WAS SO WORRIED ABOUT AYANNA, SHE DIDN'T REALIZE IT.

SHE'LL BE ALL RIGHT...

RIGHT?

THE RHYTHM, THE WIND... IT'S ALL *WRONG.* THAT HOLE IN THE SKY IS TURNING THIS WORLD INSIDE OUT.

WHATEVER POISON THOSE IRON BUGS PUT IN THEIR *SOULS,* IT'S BEYOND MY CONJURE. I KNOW SOME FOLK WHO CAN HELP. IF WE MAKE IT IN TIME.

*TALK* TO YOUR FRIENDS. DISTRACT THEM FROM THE PAIN.

AYANNA, I'M SURE TO YOU IT LOOKS LIKE I'M ALWAYS TRYING TOO HARD TO BE A HERO. IT'S. . . IT'S BECAUSE THE ONE TIME I SHOULD'VE SAVED SOMEONE, I PANICKED. I *MESSED UP,* AND MY FRIEND. . . HE DIED. THAT FAILURE HAUNTS ME EVERY NIGHT.

IT WAS LAST WINTER. WE WERE COMING BACK FROM A FIELD TRIP WHEN THE BUS HIT A PATCH OF ICE. WE SWERVED INTO THE PATH OF A TRUCK. THE IMPACT SMASHED THE REAR OF THE BUS AND PUSHED US OVER THE EDGE OF A BRIDGE.

I MADE IT OUT, BUT. . . EDDIE WAS STUCK BETWEEN TWO SEATS. "TRISTAN, PULL ME OUT. TRISTAN. TRISTAN." I STILL HEAR HIS VOICE.

BUT I WAS SO *SCARED.* SCARED OF FALLING. I DIDN'T WANT TO DIE. EDDIE WAS CALLING ME, AND ALL I COULD THINK ABOUT WAS I DIDN'T WANT TO DIE.

SOME HERO, RIGHT?

THE ELDERS SAY PAIN IS THE BODY'S WAY OF SAYING IT'S HEALING. YOU HAVE TO LET YOURSELF HEAL.

TOO MUCH IS THE SAME AS NOT ENOUGH. BE SAD, BUT DON'T BE TOO SAD.

EVERYONE HOLD ON BACK THERE.

"WE'VE ARRIVED."

HOW WILL THIS HELP AYANNA? WE'VE ALREADY BEEN TO THE GOLDEN CRESCENT. THE CITY IS EMPTY.

THERE'S NO PEOPLE, BUT THAT DOESN'T MEAN IT'S EMPTY.

...TRISTAN?

I'M RIGHT HERE.

THEY'VE AGREED TO HELP. BUT ONLY AYANNA AND CHESTNUTT CAN STAY.

WE MUST GO NOW. THEY'RE GETTING *AGITATED*, AND YOU DON'T WANT TO ANGER THE MMOATIA.

I'M COMING BACK. SO DON'T YOU DARE GO ANYWHERE.

WHERE'D YOU LEARN TO SPEAK WHISTLE?

I STUDIED UNDER THEM FOR MANY YEARS.

TIME'S GETTING THIN. THE RIP HAS NEARLY REACHED THE MAINLAND.

THEN LET'S DO WHAT WE CAME TO DO.

LET'S GET THE STORY BOX FIXED.

"THE *RIGHT* ONE IS WAITING."

TRISTAN! I DON'T KNOW WHAT YOU DID, BUT I'M FIXING TO SLAP YOUR BACK UNTIL MORNING, BOY. YOU *SAVED* US ALL!

*WELL DONE*, YOUNG STRONG.

WELL, KISS MY WRIST, I BET YOU THINK YOU'RE *HOT STUFF* NOW.

AND LOOK WHO'S ALL BETTER. THE MMOATIA WORKED NONSTOP TO HELP THEM RECOVER.

I TOLD YOU NOT TO START A WAR, FLYBOY.

YOU GOT RID OF THE MAAFA AND *FREED* ALL THE CAPTIVES! YUP, YUP!

THAT'S *QUITE ENOUGH* CELEBRATING.

MANY, MANY, *MANY* MISTAKES WERE MADE. CHIEF AMONG THEM WAS NOT BRINGING THE STORY BOX STRAIGHT BACK TO *ME*.

HAD YOU DONE WHAT I ASKED, THIS UNNECESSARY *VIOLENCE* WOULD HAVE BEEN PREVENTED.

NOW, IF YOU'LL HAND OVER THAT STORY BOX, I WILL START FIXING THE MESS YOU CAUSED WITH THAT *TEMPER* OF YOURS.

I'M NOT GIVING IT TO YOU. YOU'RE THE *WRONG* ONE.

"YOU WILL *ALWAYS* BE WELCOME HERE."

CRAZY AS IT SOUNDS, I'LL MISS THIS PLACE.

ENOUGH WITH THE SAPPY WORDS, OR GUM BABY'S GONNA START CRYING. *NOBODY* WANTS THAT.

YOU CAN COME BACK FOR MY WARREN SOCIETY INITIATION CEREMONY, TRISTAN. AFTER ALL THE KNOWLEDGE I LEARNED ON OUR TRAVELS, THEY'RE GONNA MAKE ME A *FULL MEMBER!*

FAREWELL, TRISTAN. I WILL TELL YOUR STORY TO THE ELDERS.

AND YOU WILL BE ADMITTED TO ISIHLANGU WITH *OPEN ARMS* AT ANY TIME.

RECKON I MIGHT HAMMER TOGETHER A *BRIDGE* BETWEEN HERE AND MIDPASS. SEE IF WE CAN'T LEARN TO GET ALONG BETTER WITH THE *CITY FOLK.*

YOU BE SAFE NOW, CHAMP. I'LL MISS HAVING YOU AROUND.

BYE, FLYBOY.

LATER, PILOT.

OLD FAMILIAR IS READY TO SCOOT YOU *HOME*, KID.

Copyright © 2022 by Cake Creative

All rights reserved. Published by Disney • Hyperion, an imprint of Buena Vista Books, Inc. No part of this book may be reproduced or transmitted in any form or by any means, electronic or mechanical, including photocopying, recording, or by any information storage and retrieval system, without written permission from the publisher. For information address Disney • Hyperion, 77 West 66th Street, New York, New York 10023.

First Edition, August 2022
10 9 8 7 6 5 4 3 2 1
FAC-038091-2132
Printed in the United States of America

This book is set in Ask for Mercy, Sans Sanity BB, and Dearly Departed/Fontspring
Designed by Tyler Nevins
Illustrations by Olivia Stephens
Color by Laura Langston, with additional color by Paris Alleyne
Lettering by Ariana Maher

Library of Congress Cataloging-in-Publication Control Number: 2022932651

Hardcover ISBN 978-1-368-07280-9
Paperback ISBN 978-1-368-07500-8

Reinforced binding for hardcover edition

Visit www.DisneyBooks.com
Follow @ReadRiordan